*"He thought in other heads—
and in his own, others besides
himself thought."*
Bertolt Brecht

KING PIN

New *ZIPPY* strips

by Bill Griffith

E. P. DUTTON • NEW YORK

Published in the United States by E.P. Dutton, a division of NAL Penguin Inc., 2 Park Avenue, New York, N.Y. 10016.

Published simultaneously in Canada by Fitzhenry and Whiteside, Limited, Toronto.

Library of Congress Catalog Card Number: 87-70957

ISBN: 0-525-48330-6
Book design and production: Bill Griffith
Typography: Ampersand Design
Camera Work: G. Howard, Inc.

W

10 9 8 7 6 5 4 3 2 1

First Edition

Respectfully dedicated to

"ZIP THE WHAT-IS-IT?"

(William Henry Jackson)

1842-1926

ZIPPY — "LUNATIC" — BILL GRIFFITH

ZIPPY — "MAKE MINE GLAZED" — BILL GRIFFITH

ZIPPY "THE TERRIBLE TWOS" BILL GRIFFITH

Panel 1:
LET'S **GO**, ZIPPY!! THIS WAY! IT'S **FUN**! FOLLOW ME!!

OKAY, **BABY RONNIE**.. AS LONG AS YOUR RATINGS ARE HIGH!

6.25

Panel 2:
THIS ISN'T GOING TO INVOLVE TH' **TRULY NEEDY** OR **AIRLINE DE-REGULATION**, IS IT, BABY RONNIE?

WELL, I DON'T KNOW.. ..I LET **BABY MEESE** MAKE THOSE DECISIONS..

© 1986 Bill Griffith. World rights reserved. Distributed by King Features Syndicate

Panel 3:
YOW! WE'RE AT TH' EDGE OF A BIG **CLIFF!** JUST LIKE IN THE **ROAD RUNNER!** I'D SIGN A **PEACE TREATY** IF I COULD READ!!

I LIKE TO CRAWL OUT HERE & STARE OVER THE **EDGE**..I ASKED **BABY GORBACHEV** TO COME TOO, BUT HIS **COUNTRY** WOULDN'T LET HIM..

Panel 4:
C'MON!! LET'S THROW **TEMPER TANTRUMS** AND HOLD OUR **BREATH** 'TIL **1988**!!

I CAN'T... I LENT MY **TACTICAL NUCLEAR RATTLE** TO THE **BABY JOINT CHIEFS OF STAFF** & THEY WON'T GIVE IT **BACK**!!

ZIPPY "YOUR SERVE" BILL GRIFFITH

Panel 1:
BLAUPUNKT..

BLAUPUNKT.

Panel 2:
BLAUPUNKT.

BLAUPUNKT.

Panel 3:
BLAUPUNKT.

BLAUPUNKT.

© 1986 Bill Griffith. World rights reserved. Distributed by King Features Syndicate

6-26

Panel 4:
...LANGUAGE IS **PING-PONG**!!

WHO WON?

ZIPPY "TO PROVE A POINT" BILL GRIFFITH

DR. MARVIN LIPSCHITZ CONDUCTS A SERIES OF **TESTS**..

ALL RIGHT, ZIPPY.. I'M HOLDING UP 8 BY 10 GLOSSIES OF **CONWAY TWITTY** AND **HENRY KISSINGER**..WHAT'S TH' **CONNECTION**?

GRIFFITH

6·27

IT WAS JUNE OF **1959** & HENRY WAS ON A TRAIN GOING THROUGH **TUSCALOOSA, ALABAMA**..CONWAY WAS JUST GETTING OUT OF THE **AIR FORCE**..

UH-HUH..

THEY MET IN TH' **CLUB CAR**.. YOU HAVE TO REMEMBER, "**TWITTY CITY**" WAS JUST A **DREAM** AT THAT TIME.. AND NEWS OF TH' **MID-EAST CRISIS** HADN'T EVEN REACHED TH' **MID-WEST!!**

I SEE..

TH' **TRAIN LURCHED** AS IT PULLED INTO **LARCHMONT**, SPILLING HENRY'S **SCRABBLE BOARD** ON CONWAY'S **GUITAR CASE**... TH' WORDS "**BUY 40 ACRES OUTSIDE NASHVILLE**" WERE FORMED &, OF COURSE, 18 YEARS LATER WE HAD TH' **ARAB OIL EMBARGO!**

NEXT, WE HAVE **RALPH NADER** & **RONA BARRETT!!**

© 1986 Bill Griffith. World rights reserved. Distributed by King Features Syndicate

ZIPPY "PERSPIRATION" BILL GRIFFITH

GRIFFY, THIS IS YOUR **4,728**TH COMIC STRIP!! **WHERE** DO YOU GET ALL YOUR **IDEAS??**

WELL..THERE'S THIS **LAUNDROMAT** IN **ORLANDO**..

6·30

I **KNEW** IT.. TH' **SPIN CYCLE**..

EVERY TUESDAY AFTERNOON, I RECEIVE A **CODED TELEX** FROM THIS GUY.. CALL HIM "**ELMER**"..THE STRIPS ARE COMPLETELY WRITTEN OUT.. HE EVEN SENDS DETAILED **PENCIL DRAWINGS**--

ALL **I** HAVE TO DO IS CHECK FOR **TYPOS** AND **LIBEL**, THEN **INK** 'EM.. ..THIS HAS BEEN GOING ON FOR CLOSE TO **SEVENTEEN YEARS**.. Y'KNOW, IT FEELS GOOD TO FINALLY **TELL** SOMEONE ---

SO **THAT** EXPLAINS THE **FERRARIS** & **TAHITIAN** VACATIONS!!

..SIGH.. IF IT WAS ONLY **TRUE** HUH, ZIP??

YOU **MEAN** THERE'S NO SUCH PLACE AS **ORLANDO?**

© 1986 Bill Griffith. World rights reserved. Distributed by King Features Syndicate

ZIPPY — "MARITAL AIDS" — BILL GRIFFITH

Panel 1: I'M HEAD OVER EELS IN *LOVE* WITH MY "PULSE-MATIC" *OSTERIZER*..WE HAVE A *16-SPEED* RELATIONSHIP...

Panel 2: YES.. THERE'S *NO WAY* ANYTHING COULD COME BETWEEN ME AND MY SIMULATED WOOD GRAIN, DE LUXE *TOAST-R-OVEN!!*

Panel 3: EVERY EVENING, I TENDERLY *TUCK IN* MY BELOVED WEST BEND "STIR CRAZY" *POPCORN POPPER*... I'M SO GRATEFUL FOR ITS BIGGER, *FLUFFIER KERNELS*..

Panel 4: ..AND WHEN I AWAKEN EACH MORNING, THERE IT IS, *DRIPPING SOFTLY* BESIDE ME, ITS "ULTRONIC BREW CYCLE" TOTALLY IN TUNE WITH MY OWN--- MY LITTLE *"MR. COFFEE"*...

..WHO WAS THAT *CROCK-POT* I SAW YOU WITH LAST NIGHT??

ZIPPY — "RUSSIAN SKEEBALL" — BILL GRIFFITH

Panel 1: HEY, I DIDN'T KNOW YOU WERE A *VODKA* MAN, ZIP.. WHAT'S WITH TH' *VAST QUANTITIES??*

IT'S A *PERSONAL* THING, SHELF-LIFE!!

Panel 2: I HAVE TO *PROTECT* MYSELF...

PROTECT? FROM WHAT? A *GIN* & *TONIC* INVASION FROM AN ALIEN PLANET??

Panel 3: LISTEN, ANOTHER DETAIL, WHY ONLY *"SMIRNOFF"?* I DIDN'T NOTICE ANY *CONTESTS* ON TH' LABEL..

IT *HAS* TO BE *SMIRNOFF*, S.L.-- I'M *ALLERGIC!!*

Panel 4: *ALLERGIC?* WHAT COULD YOU POSSIBLY BE *ALLERGIC* TO THAT *SMIRNOFF* WOULD HELP?

SMIRNS.

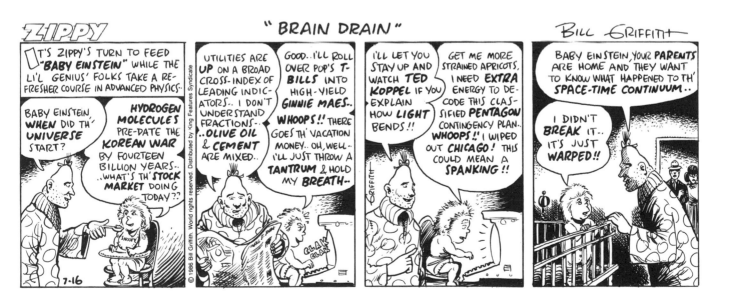

ZIPPY

"HOLDING COURT"

Bill Griffith

Panel 1:

THE TIME IS **2020**, ZIPPY'S EYESIGHT IS **80/80** AND HIS **SAGE ADVICE** IS SOUGHT BY SHELF-LIFE'S TROUBLED SON, **"POP ROX"!**

ZIPPY, MY LIFE IS A **MESS**.. I'M **BUYING**, I'M **SELLING**.. BUT I'M NOT EN-JOYING!

STOP & **SMELL** TH' **CONCRETE**, MY BOY..

Panel 2:

"SMELL TH' **CONCRETE**"? YOU **KNOW** WE'RE NOT ALLOWED OUTSIDE.. THIS DARN "NUCLEAR WINTER" GIVES ME A **PAIN!**

FLORIDA IS NICE.. IF YOU WEAR YOUR **LEAD-LINED** SUN-BONNET!

ACME MODULAR BUBBLE UNIT 303

DANGER: GARBAGE

Panel 3:

WHAT D'YOU THINK OF THESE NEW "**RENT-AN EMOTION**" OUTLETS? MAYBE I COULD TRY "**SELF PITY**" OR "**ENNUI**" FOR A WEEK.. WOULD IT **HELP**??

LIFE IS NOT WORTH LIVING IF YOU DON'T HAVE A **BATTERY** OF HIGH-POWERED ATTORNEYS!!

HERE.. TAKE **THIS**..

7·21

Panel 4:

A **BATTERY** OF HIGH-POWERED ATTORNEYS!! THAT'S TH' **TICKET**!! I COULD **LITIGATE** MY WAY TO TOTAL **SELF-FULFILLMENT**! HEY, WHAT'S THIS OFFICIAL-LOOKING **DOCUMENT**?

IT'S A **SUMMONS**.. I'M **SUING** YOU FOR **TRESPASS**, **THEFT** OF **SERVICES** & **WHIPLASH**!!

ZIPPY

"TOO CUTE FOR COMFORT"

Bill Griffith

Panel 1:

7·22

Panel 2:

EXCUSE ME, BUT AREN'T YOU THAT ZANY, MISCHIEVOUS **CARTOON CHARACTER** BELOVED BY MILLIONS **COAST TO COAST**?

NO.. I WAS **BORN** LIKE THIS AND I'D APPRECIATE IT IF YOU'D **MIND** YOUR OWN **BUSINESS**..

NUDGE

Panel 3:

I'M **SORRY**.. I THOUGHT THIS WAS A **WACKY**, OUTRAGEOUS NEW COMIC STRIP...

JEEZ...

ZIPPY   "NO PROBLEM"   BILL GRIFFITH

ZIPPY, ARE YOU MAKING TH' **SANDWICHES** FOR TH' COMPANY **PICNIC**??

YES, I AM CREATING MANY MULTI-LAYERED **FOODSTUFFS**..

WHAT **KIND** ARE YOU MAKING??

COOL WHIP AND **SLICED BEETS** ON **FRENCH ROLL**..

DON'T YOU THINK MAYBE THAT'S A LITTLE TOO **EXOTIC** FOR TH' GUYS AT **WORK**?

OKAY, I'LL USE **WHOLE WHEAT**!!

7·25

ZIPPY   "FREE ENTERPRISE"   BILL GRIFFITH

S.L.!! WHY ARE YOU SO UPSET? DID **BEEDLEBAUM** COME IN LAST AT **HIALEAH**?

WORSE..I'VE GOT **40,000** BEEF PATTIES IN TH' SHAPE OF TH' **STATUE OF LIBERTY** THAT DIDN'T SELL..

MAYBE YOU SHOULD CALL IN TO A **RADIO TALK SHOW** & CONFESS YOUR FAILING TO **THOUSANDS** OF STRANGERS!

..I CAN'T FIGURE IT.. SOME GUY IN NEW YORK DID A SIXTY POUND **CHOPPED LIVER STATUE OF LIBERTY**...IT WAS A **SENSATION**!! WHERE DID I GO **WRONG**?

BIG BUX

7·28

I'M WEARING **STATUE OF LIBERTY PEEK·A·BOO BOXER SHORTS**.. THEY'RE IMPORTED!!

..THIS IS EVEN A BIGGER **FIASCO** THAN THOSE **20,000 FOAM** REPLICAS OF **HALLEY'S COMET** I HAD MADE UP.

GEE, S.L... I THOUGHT THERE WAS ALWAYS A **BRIGHT SIDE** TO EVERY **DISMAL & DEPRESSING** SITUATION!!

THERE **IS** — AT LEAST YOU KNOW WHAT'S FOR **SUPPER** FOR TH' NEXT **54 YEARS**..

PASS TH' **HUDDLED MASSES**..

ZIPPY

"FEELINGS-Я-US"

BILL GRIFFITH

CLAUDE, **WHY** IS THERE A BIG **HOLE** IN YOUR LIVING-ROOM **WALL**? IS A LARGE **MARSUPIAL** FROM **LATVIA** ON TH' LOOSE?

NO, LI'L BUDDY.. IT'S THERE 'CAUSE I GOT SO **MAD** AT SOMEBODY, I HAD T' PUNCH **SOMETHIN'**.

WELL, WHY DIDN'T YOU PUNCH TH' PERSON WHO **MADE** YOU ANGRY? DON'T YOU WATCH THE **A-TEAM**?

LIFE AIN'T NO **TV SHOW**, LI'L BUDDY.. WHEN SOMEONE **LIES** TO YOU OR DOES YOU **WRONG**, YOU GOTTA ACT LIKE A **ADULT** & MAKE THEM UN'ER-STAN' YOUR POSITION.

IS THAT WHY YOU'RE CLUTCHING AN **UZI SUBMACHINE GUN** TENDERLY TO YOUR BREAST?

I WONDER IF I SHOULD GO FOR TH' **KNEECAPS** OR JUST BLOW AWAY HIS **3-PIECE SUIT**??

7-31

© 1986 Bill Griffith. World rights reserved. Distributed by King Features Syndicate

---

ZIPPY

"POWER FAILURE"

BILL GRIFFITH

SHELF-LIFE, **WHY** IS THAT BALD GUY **SNOOZING** WHILE TH' **CONTRAS** SPEND OUR **HUNDRED MILLION DOLLARS** ON PARTY SUPPLIES??

HE'S **NOT** ASLEEP, ZIPPY-HE'S "**CHANNELING**".. KIND OF LIKE HE'S **POSSESSED**..

8-1

"**CHANNELING**"? WHERE'S HIS **REMOTE CONTROL**?

HE'S IN CONTACT WITH A **NONPHYSICAL ENTITY** FROM HALFWAY ACROSS TH' **UNIVERSE**!!

© 1986 Bill Griffith. World rights reserved. Distributed by King Features Syndicate

JEEZ, **NOW** WHAT ARE YOU DOING??

"**CHANNELING**," OF COURSE..

SMURF

OH, YEH? **WHO'S** COMING THROUGH? THE ANGUISHED SOUL OF **WARD CLEAVER**?

NO-- I'M IN CONTACT WITH A **PHYSICAL NON-ENTITY** FROM ACROSS TH' **STREET**!!

ZIPPY

"PROPHET and LOSS"

BILL GRIFFITH

ZIPPY

"WILD IMPULSES: NEXT 3,000 MILES"

BILL GRIFFITH

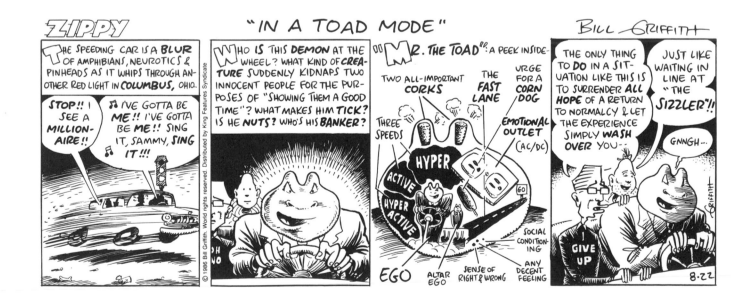

ZIPPY   "TOAD AWAY"   BILL GRIFFITH

MR. TOAD & HIS KIDNAPED CARGO TOOL INTO *TRENTON, NEW JERSEY,* WITH A *SONG* IN THEIR *HEARTS* & A *TRAFFIC COP* ON THEIR *TAIL*..

ISN'T *NEW JERSEY* WHERE TH' LAUNDRO-MATS *HAVE TO* BE OPEN *24 HRS.* A DAY?

I JUST HEARD A *SNAP*.. I LOST IT.. IT'S *HISTORY*...MY *MIND* IS *HISTORY*..

OKAY, BOYS!! *LAST STOP!!* I KNOW TH' *GOVERNOR* PERSONALLY!! *LOAN* ME ANOTHER TWENTY, HUH??

YOU TWO WAIT HERE-- I'VE GOT A SUDDEN *URGE* TO *MERGE* WITH A *CHEESE-STEAK* & A *CRISP, FULL-BODIED* PINT OF *THUNDERBIRD!*

LOOK, S.L.!! *STATE-OF-THE-ART SPEED DRYERS!!*

LAUNDRO WORLD
GONE.. ALL GONE..

BIG ZERO

OVER 21

© 1986 Bill Griffith. World rights reserved. Distributed by King Features Syndicate

9-1

YOW, S.L.!! IT'S *CRISP* & *FULL-BODIED* IN *HERE,* TOO! PLUS, I CAN SEE THE EN-TIRE *CAST* OF *DYNASTY* AND *RON REAGAN, JR.* IN A *PINK TU-TU!!* IT MUST BE TH' *SIXTH DIMENSION!*

SOUNDS GOOD.. DO THEY TAKE *AMERICAN EXPRESS?*

SUDS 'N' SUBS

NUTS BOY

MORE, MORE, MORE!!

ZIPPY   "MONDO BIZARRO"   BILL GRIFFITH

ZIPPY & *SHELF-LIFE* ENTER THE *6TH DIMENSION,* FOL-LOWED CLOSELY BY *MR. TOAD*--

THIS ISN'T *TRENTON!!*

WHY DO I SUDDENLY WANT TO *DO-NATE* ALL MY TIME & MONEY TO *CHARITY?*

BE NICE

AND WHY DO *I* SUDDENLY FEEL TH' NEED TO EX-PRESS MY *TENDER FEELINGS* ABOUT *SOFT, PLUSH TOYS* & *FLORAL ARRANGEMENTS?*

MAYBE I'LL ADOPT 14 TINY *ORPHANS* AND TELL THEM ABOUT *WALT DISNEY!*

?

THANK YOU

9-2

I *WUV SNOOPY!*

DR. RUTH IS *CUTE..*

EXCUSE ME, BUT WHY DO *I* SUDDENLY WANT TO ENROLL IN *POST-GRADUATE LAW STUDIES??*

BECAUSE YOU'RE ALL IN THE *6TH DI-*MENSION WHERE *EVERYTHING* IS *RE-VERSED!!*

6

CARL SAGAN DROPPED IN LAST WEEK AND NOW HE DRIVES A *PICKUP* AND HUNTS SMALL, *DEFENSELESS ANIMALS!!*

I THINK I'LL READ *"WAR AND PEACE"* COVER-TO-COVER IN *ONE SITTING,* RIGHT AFTER I GET *MARRIED,* MOVE TO DEN-VER & GROW A *MOUSTACHE!*

© 1986 Bill Griffith. World rights reserved. Distributed by King Features Syndicate

ZIPPY "A DIET THAT WORKS" BILL GRIFFITH

CLAUDE'S **MISSION**: RESCUE ZIPPY AND COMPANY FROM THE CLUTCHES OF **STEVEN SPIELBERG** & THE **6TH DIMENSION**..

STEVE, **BABE**, I JUST HEARD ABOUT 3 **SUBURBANITES** WHO SWEAR THEY HAVE PROOF **DONNIE OSMOND** IS FROM **JUPITER**!

WHERE? **WHERE**? ..ARE THEY **OPTIONED**??

WHO IS THIS **LOUT**?

OKAY, L'IL BUDDY, I WANT YOU TO SCARF DOWN SEVERAL DOZEN O' THESE FINE **HOSTESS** PRODUCTS... IT'S TH' ONLY THING'LL **RESTORE** YOU TO YOUR OL' **ZANY** SELF!!

SURELY, YOU **JEST**... NO **ARTIFICIAL INGREDIENT** SHALL EVER **SULLY** TH' SACRED PORTALS OF MY REFINED **DIGESTIVE TRACT**!!

YOUR **LUNCH** IS IN THE **MAIL**!!

Hostess THIS SIDE UP

3 HOURS & **32** DOZEN DINGDONGS LATER..

MMM.. NOT BAD..

ALL RIGHT, **ONE MORE** BITE.. NOW WHAT WERE TH' **NAMES** OF THE "**JETSON**" KIDS??

GNRB.. BLUH.. ..UM.. JUDY?? JUDY & ELROY!!!

THAT'S MY **ZIPPY**!!

ZIPPY "GREAT SLATE FOR '88?" BILL GRIFFITH

CLAUDE'S MIRACLE "**HOSTESS DIET**" HAS BROUGHT **ZIPPY** & S.L. BACK FROM THE **6TH DIMENSION** BUT IT'S HAVING A STRANGE EFFECT ON **MR. TOAD**...

MUST BE TH' "**MODIFIED FOOD STARCH**"!

YES.. I'LL START A NEW **RELIGION**.. NO.. A NEW **POLITICAL PARTY**.. NO.. I'LL COMBINE THE TWO!!

Hostess WITH THE Mostess

NOW HE'S GOT THIS **UNCONTROLLABLE URGE** TO BE **PRESIDENT** OF TH' **UNITED STATES**!!

YEH.. BUT FIRST HE SAID HE WANTS TO TALK TO TH' **POPE** ABOUT "**COSTUME DESIGN**"..

WELL, AT LEAST **YOU** TWO FELLAS ARE BACK TO **NORMAL**... YOU'RE NOT PLANNIN' ON RUNNIN' FOR **POLITICAL OFFICE** IN TH' NEAR FUTURE ARE YA? HEH-HEH---

9.1

MR. TOAD! WAIT!! I KNOW LYNDON LAROUCHE'S **MASTERCARD** NUMBER!

AND I CAN'T EVEN PRONOUNCE "**CHAPPAQUIDDICK**"!

OY.

ZIPPY — "A SPREE" — BILL GRIFFITH

Panel 1:
CHECK IT OUT, ZIPPY.. THERE GOES A GUY STILL WEARING **BELL BOTTOMS**! HOW COULD HE BE SO **UNAWARE**?

MAYBE HE DOESN'T HAVE AN "ESPRIT" CATALOG..

Panel 2:
I HAVE TO ADMIT EVEN **I'VE** GOTTEN INTO THE **TAPERED LEG** LOOK.. ALTHOUGH I STEADFASTLY **REFUSE** TO WEAR RUNNING SHOES WITH **VELCRO FLAPS**!

THEY **WON'T** LET YOU INTO BURGER KING WITHOUT **MULTIPLE VELCRO SHOE FLAPS**!!

Panel 3:
Y'KNOW, THIS WHOLE **BIG SHOULDER, TIGHT ANKLE, PRIMARY-COLOR** THING WILL LOOK ABSOLUTELY **RIDICULOUS** TEN YEARS FROM NOW!!

YES, **FASHIONS** COME AND GO, BUT A **LAVA LAMP** IS FOREVER!!

I LOOK GOOD...

10-14

ZIPPY — "BURNED AGAIN" — BILL GRIFFITH

Panel 1:
THAT'S TH' GUY, ZIP.. **PAT ROBERTSON**.. HE SAYS TH' MAN UPSTAIRS WANTS HIM T' BE **PRESIDENT**!!

WHATEVER **MR. FEENEY** SAYS IS ALL **RIGHT** WITH ME!!

Panel 2:
HE SAYS THERE'S NOTHIN' BUT A **FINE LINE** BETWEEN TH' **CHURCH** AND TH' **STATE**.. --I DON' KNOW..

THERE'S AN EVEN **FINER** LINE BETWEEN **JAMES REHNQUIST** AND **YOGI BERRA**!!

10-15

Panel 3:
'COURSE, HE ALSO USE'TA DO A BIT O' **FAITH HEALIN',** AND I GOT THIS PAINFUL, ITCHY **BUNION**... SO I MAY VOTE FOR TH' GUY..

CAN HE PREDICT **HAILSTORMS**?

Panel 4:
WELL, HE **DID** ALTER TH' COURSE O' **HURRICANE GLORIA** A WHILE BACK..

GOOD.. **I'LL** VOTE FOR HIM, TOO-- AS SOON AS IT **SNOWS** IN **FORT LAUDERDALE**!!

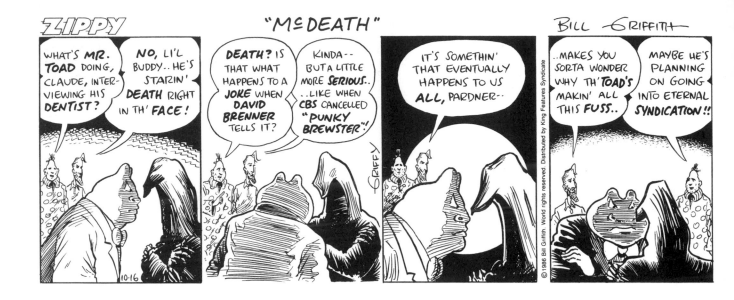

ZIPPY

"BOWLED OVER"

BILL GRIFFITH

ZIPPY!! YOU'VE GOT A **SEVEN-TEN** SPLIT!! THROW IT, AWREADY!! THERE'S **DOUGH** RIDING ON THIS GAME!

— HEY, **C'MON!!** YOU'RE NOT S'POSED TO HAVE A **RELATIONSHIP** WITH TH' BALL! JUST **TOSS** IT, WILL YA?!!

© 1986 Bill Griffith. World rights reserved. Distributed by King Features Syndicate

10·20

I'M **SORRY**... I JUST REALIZED THAT TH' **UNIVERSE** HAS NO **BEGINNING** OR **END** & **LIFE** & **DEATH** ARE SIMPLY STAGES IN AN ENDLESS CYCLE OF **HARMONY**, **ORDER** AND **DANIELLE STEELE NOVELS**·

ZIPPY

"SPACE TRAVEL"

BILL GRIFFITH

WHAT DO YOU WANNA DO **NOW**, ZIPPY??

OH, GATHER SAMPLES OF **LICHEN** & **HYDROGEN** MOLECULES, I GUESS--

© 1986 Bill Griffith. World rights reserved. Distributed by King Features Syndicate

10·21

WHAT ABOUT GRABBIN' A **FALAFEL**.. OR SOME **SUSHI**?

I WILL BE GLAD TO **ANALYZE** THESE UNKNOWN SUBSTANCES..

WE COULD HOP IN TH' **HYUNDAI** & PICK UP TH' LATEST "**TALKING HEADS**" ALBUM!

HEY, IT'S **YOUR** PLANET!

WHY DO I GET TH' FEELING YOU'RE TREATING ME LIKE A **MAN FROM MARS** TODAY??

I NEVER MET AN **ALIEN LIFE FORM** I DIDN'T LIKE!!

ZIPPY   "FESTIVE OCCASION"   BILL GRIFFITH

LET'S **GO, ZIP** — WE'RE GONNA BE LATE FOR TH' **PARTY**.. WHERE'S YOUR **COSTUME**?

BE RIGHT WITH YOU, CLAUDE.. I'M WRAPPING SHELF-LIFE'S TWELVE-PAK OF "**MIRACLE WHIP**"!

10·31

FOR CRYIN' OUT LOUD, ZIP... WHAT'RE YOU DOIN' GIVIN' **GIFTS** ON **OCTOBER 31ST**??

'TIS TH' **SEASON** TO BE **JOLLY**!!

THIS AIN'T **CHRISTMAS**, OL' BUDDY!! WE'RE CELEBRATIN' **HALLOWEEN**!!

APRIL FOOLS'!!

© 1986 Bill Griffith. World rights reserved. Distributed by King Features Syndicate

---

ZIPPY   "TRANSCENDENTAL MEDICATION"   BILL GRIFFITH

ZIPPY, IS THERE A **GREAT MYSTERY** YOU WISH TO FATHOM? AN UNKNOWABLE **UNKNOWABLENESS** BEYOND ALL REASON?

YES...

11·3

© 1986 Bill Griffith. World rights reserved. Distributed by King Features Syndicate

...DI-GEL.

"DI-GEL"?

WHAT **SPECIFICALLY** IS IT ABOUT THIS "**DI-GEL**" THAT YOU WISH TO COMPREHEND?

GAS-CALMING **SIMETHICONE**...

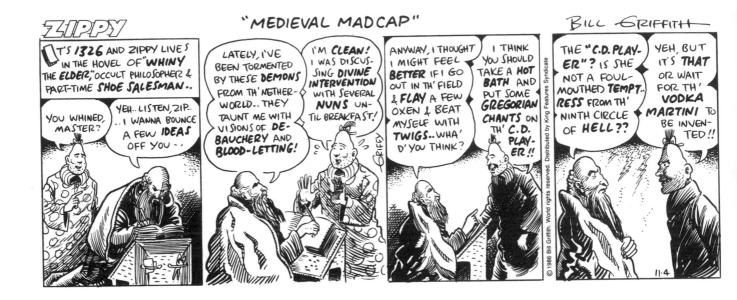

ZIPPY — "LARGE CHARGE" — BILL GRIFFITH

I'M HAVING A HORRIBLE NIGHTMARE-- *JANE FONDA* "WORK-OUTS" ARE SPRINGING UP EVERYWHERE.. ..*PAUL NEWMAN* LEERS AT ME FROM JARS OF INDUSTRIAL-STRENGTH *SPAGHETTI SAUCE*..

CYBILL SHEPHERD WANTS MY *HAIR* TO *GLOW*.. *BILL COSBY* SAYS *JELL-O* WILL MAKE ME YOUNG AGAIN, AND *ELI WALLACH'S* NEW YORK ACCENT ECHOS IN MY HEAD EACH TIME I ENTER A *NISSAN* SHOWROOM..

BEFORE I FALL *ASLEEP* NEXT TIME, I'D BETTER CHECK TH' *CREDIT LIMIT* ON MY *AMERICAN EXPRESS CARD*!!

KARL MALDEN'S NOSE

© 1986 Bill Griffith. World rights reserved. Distributed by King Features Syndicate

---

ZIPPY — "CHILDREN OF ALL AGES" — BILL GRIFFITH

ZIPPY & CLAUDE ARE PLAYING "LAZER TAG" AT THEIR NEIGHBORHOOD TAVERN--

EAT *INFRA-RED* STAR-LIGHT, *DING-DONG* BREATH!!

TASTE SUBLIMATED *YUPPIE ANGST*, TRAILER TRASH!!

DIRECT *HIT* ON YOUR *STAR-SENSOR*, DWEEB-DOME!!

YOW!! NOW I UNDER-STAND ADVANCED *MICROBIOLOGY* AND TH' NEW *TAX REFORM* LAWS!!

BRRRT!! BIP!!

YOU *DO*? MAYBE YOU COULD EXPLAIN HOW THEY'D AFFECT A SINGLE-INCOME, *DIVORCED MALE* WITH ITEMIZED DEDUCTIONS-

FOOLED YOU! ABSORB *EGO SHAT-TERING* IM-PULSE RAYS, POLYESTER *POLTROON*!!

BRRRT! BIP!!

LET'S TAKE A *BREAK*, ZIP.. I'M SUDDENLY *OVERWHELMED* BY A SENSE OF MY OWN *MORTALITY*..

YOU MEAN NOW I CAN'T *SHOOT YOU* IN TH' BACK AND FURTHER *BLUR* TH' DISTINCTION BETWEEN *FANTASY* & *REALITY*?

© 1986 Bill Griffith. World rights reserved. Distributed by King Features Syndicate

ZIPPY "OPTIMISM" BILL GRIFFITH

ZIPPY, SHELF-LIFE TELLS ME YOU FEEL SO *GOOD* ABOUT *CALVIN KLEIN'S* *"OBSESSION,"* YOU CAN'T STOP REPEATING TH' SAME SENTENCE OVER & OVER--

WE HAVE A JACK-KNIFED *BIG RIG* ON INTERSTATE *80*...

PERSONALLY, I FIND *ANYTHING* ASSOCIATED WITH *CALVIN KLEIN* TO BE A GREAT CAUSE FOR *EMBARRASSMENT*..

WE HAVE A JACK-KNIFED *BIG RIG* ON INTERSTATE *80*...

ANYWAY, I'M GLAD YOU'RE *HAPPY*.. THERE'S PRECIOUS LITTLE TO FEEL *GOOD* ABOUT THESE DAYS--

WE HAVE A JACK-KNIFED *BIG RIG* ON INTERSTATE *80*...

11·12

ZIPPY "BAD TIMING" BILL GRIFFITH

WELL, YOUR *SOLENOID'S* ALL WORN OUT & TH' BRUSHES ON YOUR *ALTERNATOR* MAY BE A HAIR OFF..

A "HAIR OFF".. YEH, WHAT ELSE?

OK, YOUR *DISTRIBUTOR VACUUM ADVANCE* ISN'T ADVANCIN', YOU NEED A NEW *HEAT-RISER VALVE* AN' RE-BORED *CAMS*..

UH-HUH.. ANYTHING *MORE?*

YOU *COULD* HAVE A *BLOWN HEAD* OR A *CLUTCH RUB*.. OR, IT COULD BE THE *AIR-DOOR* ON TH' *INTAKE MANIFOLD*--

HOW IS THE *ASH TRAY* DOING?

ASH TRAY'S IN *FINE* SHAPE..

OK, CHANGE TH' *AIR FRESHENER*, INSTALL A FULL SET OF *FUZZY DICE* AND GIVE ME TH' *MANDARIN SHRIMP* & AN ORDER OF *PORK FRIED RICE!*

11·13

ZIPPY "86 THE BMW" BILL GRIFFITH

ZIPPY "EASTER ISLAND" BILL GRIFFITH

ZIPPY   "FAT CHANCE"   BILL GRIFFITH

JEEZ, ZIP, LOOKS LIKE YOU'VE PUT ON A FEW POUNDS--

I WENT ON TH' "EXISTENTIAL DESPAIR DIET!!"

I QUESTIONED MY PURPOSE IN LIFE CONTINUOUSLY FOR THREE & A HALF WEEKS--

SARTRE WOULD'VE BEEN PROUD..

FINALLY, DOM DE LOUISE APPEARED TO ME IN A TU-TU & HANDED ME A RECIPE FOR MOCHA CREAM FROSTING!!

VERY EXISTENTIAL..

SO HOW'RE YOU GONNA LOSE ALL THIS EXTRA FLAB?

NOW, I'M ON TH' "LYNDON LA ROUCHE" DIET!

WHAT'S THAT?

YOU PAY FOR ALL YOUR MEALS WITH PHONY CREDIT CARDS, THEN BLAME IT ON QUEEN ELIZABETH!

JAIL IS A GREAT PLACE TO LOSE WEIGHT!!

11-28

ZIPPY   "AND THEY DELIVER!"   BILL GRIFFITH

THE "GAS-N-GO" STATION, ASHTABULA, OHIO, 7 A.M. ---

WE MUST LOCATE A TYPICAL EARTH INHABITANT!!

WE ARE ANTHROPOLOGISTS FROM ARCTURUS-9...

Little Joe / Tony

12-1

WE HAVE REFASHIONED OUR MOLECULAR STRUCTURE INTO A NEW, HUMAN-PLEASING FORM..

OUR STUDIES SHOW THIS "PIZZA CHEF" MOTIF IS MOST REASSURING TO THE ALIENS OF THIS PLANET.

Tony

I THINK WE HAVE VISUAL CONTACT WITH AN ORGANISM NOW, TONY!

RIGHT, LITTLE JOE·· EARTH BOY! PLEASE ACCEPT OUR PEACE OFFERING OF A WARM, MOIST, GLUTENOUS DISC FROM BEYOND THE CRAB NEBULA!

DO I GET MY CHOICE OF TOPPINGS??

"STARS FROM MARS" BILL GRIFFITH

PIZZA CHEFS FROM OUTER SPACE DEBRIEF ZIPPY ABOUT **EARTH** CUSTOMS..

WE MUST NOW GET TO THE MORE **SERIOUS** QUESTIONS-- WILL **NANCY SINATRA** EVER SEE **BIG** CHART ACTION AGAIN?

SOMETIME IN 1993, **NANCY SINATRA** WILL LEAD A **BLOODLESS COUP** ON **GUAM!!**

12·4

AND **WAYNE NEWTON**... WHAT IS THE EXPLANATION FOR HIS **POWER** OVER MILLIONS?

IT'S TH' **MOUSTACHE**·· HAVE YOU EVER NOTICED TH' WAY IT RADIATES **SINCERITY, HONESTY & WARMTH?** IT'S A **MOUSTACHE** YOU WANT TO TAKE **HOME** AND INTRODUCE TO **NANCY SINATRA!**

THANK YOU, **EARTH-BOY**·· OUR MISSION IS COMPLETE·· AS A TOKEN OF APPRECIATION, WE LEAVE YOU WITH THIS PATENTED "**TRANSFORMOTRON**." PUSH THIS BUTTON & **MOAMMAR KHADAFY** BECOMES A MATCHED SET OF PLAID VINYL GARMENT BAGS!

IT'S VERY **LOVELY**·· DOES IT ALSO WORK ON **KENNY ROGERS?**

©1986 Bill Griffith. World rights reserved. Distributed by King Features Syndicate

---

ZIPPY **"PIE IN THE SKY"** BILL GRIFFITH

FAREWELL, ALIEN PIZZA CHEFS!! DON'T FORGET WHAT I TOLD YOU ABOUT **REPUBLICANS!**

OH MAN, HE'S REALLY FLIPPED HIS BOW **THIS** TIME...

JUST THINK·· WE **FINALLY** MADE CONTACT WITH **ANOTHER** INTELLIGENT SPECIES-- AND **THEY'RE** ALSO **NANCY SINATRA** FANS!!

SNIFF...

ZIP, YOU BEEN HITTIN' THAT **FERMENTED** GATOR-ADE AGAIN?

I'D **LIKE** TO BELIEVE IN FLYIN' SAUCERS **TOO**, PAL..BUT THERE'S JUS' NO **HARD EVIDENCE** T' PROVE IT!

YOU'LL **THANK** ME FOR THIS LATER, CLAUDE!!

BRRRZP!

A GIFT FROM THE SPACE BEINGS··

NOW THAT YOU'RE A 3-WAY, **ADJUSTABLE FLOOR LAMP**, DO YOU STILL INSIST **FLYING SAUCERS** ARE UNREAL?

POOF!

NO, ZIPPY, I SEE THINGS IN AN ENTIRELY **DIFFERENT LIGHT** NOW...

12·5

©1986 Bill Griffith. World rights reserved. Distributed by King Features Syndicate

ZIPPY

"DO NOT OVERLOAD THE MACHINE"

BILL GRIFFITH

Panel 1: IT'S YOUR DAY OF REST.. ..TIME TO RELAX AND DO *NOTHING*..YOU DRIFT OFF MENTALLY ON A FESTIVE, *POLYSTYRENE* AIR MATTRESS... YOUR *MIND* IS A *BLANK*.. *NO* THOUGHTS CROSS ITS PURE, STILL CALMNESS-- ...THEN, *SUDDENLY*--

WHERE DO YOUR *SOCKS* GO WHEN YOU LOSE THEM IN TH' *WASHER*?

Panel 2: *UNWANTED MUSINGS* BEGIN TO BEAT THEIR INSISTENT *TATTOO* ON YOUR HELPLESS BRAINPAN...YOU WORRY OVER LOST *CAR KEYS*, MISSED *DENTAL APPOINTMENTS* UNPAID *BILLS* AND A THOUSAND AND ONE OTHER *ARBITRARY* RUMINATIONS..

HOW MANY *RETIRED BRICK LAYERS* FROM *FLORIDA* ARE OUT PURCHASING *PENCIL SHARPENERS* RIGHT *NOW*??

12-10

Panel 3: *EASTERN MEDITATION* PRACTITIONERS TELL US WE CAN *BREAK* THIS "CHAIN OF CEASELESS THINKING" BY SIMPLY *WATCHING* EACH STRAY THOUGHT AS IT *ENTERS* AND *LEAVES* THE MIND.. THUS, WE BECOME *OBSERVERS* OF OUR OWN THOUGHTS & THEY NO LONGER TROUBLE US... WE ARE AT *PEACE* AGAIN---

UNTIL TH' *NEXT* RINSE CYCLE...

GRIFFY

ZIPPY

"LIFE GOES ON"

BILL GRIFFITH

Panel 1: *LIPPY*!! AS USUAL, YOU APPEAR TO BE *MISERABLE, DEPRESSED & UPSET*! ARE YOU HAVING *FUN* YET?

GIVE ME ONE *GOOD REASON* WHY I SHOULDN'T *END IT ALL* RIGHT HERE, SMILE FACE!!

Panel 2: WELL, HOW ABOUT TH' WAY A TIGHT *SPOTLIGHT* HITS *DOLLY PARTON'S* HIGH CHEEKBONES??

NOT GOOD ENOUGH, LAUGHING BOY!!

GRIFFY

Panel 3: WHAT ABOUT TH' SCENE IN "*CITIZEN KANE*" WHERE *ORSON WELLES* GOES BERSERK AND DESTROYS EVERYTHING IN HIS MILLION DOLLAR BEDROOM?

A *POWERFUL* PIECE OF FILMMAKING.. BUT *NOT* A REASON TO GO ON *LIVING*!

QUART O' RYE

BLEAK AIR SHAFT

12-11

Panel 4: OK, WHAT ABOUT TH' *CRASHING SURF* OUTSIDE AN *ATLANTIC CITY CASINO*? OR TH' *SMELL* OF A NEW *PONTIAC*?

BULLSEYE, ZIP.. WHA'D'YA SAY WE CRUISE TH' STRIP FOR *BURGERS*??

ZIPPY

"TAKING A CHANCE ON HAPPINESS"

BILL GRIFFITH

LIPPY & DOREEN TIE THE **KNOT** IN A BLEAK, HARSHLY LIT, **LOVELY** LAS VEGAS **WEDDING CHAPEL**...

I NOW PRONOUNCE YOU **HUSBAND** AND **WIFE**.. AND, FOR AN ADDITIONAL $49.95, WE THROW IN A VIDEOTAPE OF TH' CEREMONY.. **GOLD** EMBOSSED BOX, #3 EXTRA!

LET'S HIT TH' **TABLES**, HONEY! I FEEL **LUCKY**!

SNRK.

"BEST MAN"

MAC

SOON..

SEND MOMMA ON A **WORLD CRUISE**!!

HEY, LIPPY, DOREEN'S ALREADY LOST WHAT LITTLE **SAVINGS** YOU BOTH HAD & NOW SHE'S PLAYING ON **CREDIT**! WHAT A **DISASTER**!!

SNRK.

SHOOT!! **SNAKE-EYES** AGAIN!

IT'LL TAKE YOU **YEARS** TO PAY OFF HER **GAMBLING** DEBT!

...I **KNOW**.. MY LIFE HAS **PURPOSE** AT LAST!!

Lite

12·22

ZIPPY

"LIPPY HAS IT ALL"

BILL GRIFFITH

A STUCCO MOTEL ON THE OUTSKIRTS OF **ALBUQUERQUE**..

SOME HONEY-MOON!

INCREDIBLE.. TH' **TV'S** BUSTED, TH' ROOF **LEAKS** & THERE'S NOTHING BUT "**TUNA HELPER**" IN TH' FRIDGE..

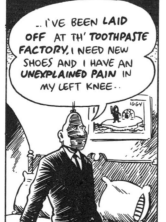

..I'VE BEEN **LAID OFF** AT TH' **TOOTHPASTE FACTORY**, I NEED NEW SHOES AND I HAVE AN **UNEXPLAINED PAIN** IN MY LEFT KNEE..

IGGY

ON TOP OF ALL THAT, I JUST MARRIED A WOMAN WHO'S **TOTALLY** OBSESSED WITH "**BIGFOOT**," AND NOW I DISCOVER SHE'S A HOPELESSLY **COMPULSIVE GAMBLER**!!

....HOW MUCH **UNMITIGATED BLISS** CAN ONE GUY TAKE??

I'M LEAVIN'!

12·23

ZIPPY

"COLOR ME CRAZY"

BILL GRIFFITH

Panel 1: GRIFFY? WHY ARE YOU COMPLETELY COVERED IN BRIGHTLY COLORED BITS OF NEWSPRINT? WERE YOU BAD?

..NEXT TIME I TRY TO START A "COLORIZING CONTEST" CHECK ME INTO TH' BETTY FORD CLINIC, WILL YOU, ZIP??

1-12

Panel 2: YOW!! PICTURES OF ME, DRESSED IN FESTIVE PURPLES, YELLOWS & GREENS! ..I DIDN'T KNOW MY LEFT KNEE WAS BLUE!

HUNDREDS OF ENTRIES!!* FROM 2-YEAR-OLDS IN OAKLAND TO ORDAINED MINISTERS IN NEW HAMPSHIRE! AND SEVERAL EVEN STAYED INSIDE TH' LINES!!

*REMEMBER THE ZIPPY COLORING CONTEST OF NOV. 18TH?

Panel 3: HOW AM I EVER GONNA DECIDE THE WINNER? HOW AM I EVER GONNA HANDLE TH' GUILT OVER TH' LOSERS? IS IT TOO LATE TO GO INTO THE VINYL SIDING BUSINESS??

LOOK AT THIS ONE! SHE SAYS IF SHE DOESN'T WIN, HER PUPPY WILL DIE!!

MORE TO COME.. &, YES, A WINNER WILL BE ANNOUNCED.. SEVERAL WINNERS.. MANY WINNERS.. HUNDREDS OF WINNERS..

ZIPPY

"CRAYONS DOWN!!"

BILL GRIFFITH

Panel 1: THE ZIPPY "COLORIZING CONTEST" CONTINUES TO HAUNT A CONFUSED CARTOONIST..

YOW!! SOME GUY IN AURORA, COLORADO, SAYS I'M A "SOUL MAN"!!

JEEZ, A CONTESTANT FROM BOSTON APPARENTLY USED PARTS FROM OLD AIR CONDITIONERS TO FASHION THIS SURREALISTIC ENTRY! WHAT A LOT O' WORK!!

ALL EXAMPLES 100% TRUE!

Panel 2: SOME ARE A TAD SCARY.. LIKE THIS ONE FROM "KEN" OF HOLLYWOOD, FL. ..HE SAYS, "I'VE BEEN COLORIZING ZIPPY FOR YEARS.. IT'S REAL GOOD THERAPY..THE DOCTORS DON'T NORMALLY ALLOW SHARP IMPLEMENTS BUT THEY MADE AN EXCEPTION.."

"SETH" FROM BROOKLINE (MA.) COLORIZED EVERY STRIP EXCEPT MINE!! IS IT CONCEPTUAL?

Panel 3: THERE REALLY ARE SOME VERY TALENTED COLORISTS.. THIS GUY FROM PALO ALTO (CA.) DID A BEAUTIFUL JOB WITH PASTELS.. VERY ARTISTIC--

WHAT ABOUT TH' POINTILLIST FROM PEABODY (MA.)??

LABOR INTENSIVE!

1·13

Panel 4: A LOT OF 'EM SENT LONG LETTERS.. "ANNIE" WANTS ME TO KNOW, "I LOOK FORWARD TO DYEING A MOP SCARLET & WEARING IT ON MY HEAD.." WHILE "MARGOT" WAXES POETIC: "YOU CAN HAVE MY ARMS, YOU CAN HAVE MY LEGS, YOU CAN HAVE MY NOSE THAT'S DRIPPY, YOU CAN HAVE MY CLOTHES, YOU CAN HAVE MY TOES, BUT MY HEART BELONGS TO ZIPPY!"

"JAMES" SAYS I'M "NAIVE YET SOCIALLY RESPONSIBLE!"

YES, WATCH THIS SPACE FOR WINNER(S)

ZIPPY

"AND THE WINNER IS..."

BILL GRIFFITH

Panel 1:
HERE IT IS, ZIP-MAN!! THE GRAND PRIZE WINNER IN TH' "ZIPPY COLORIZING CONTEST"!! IS IT NOT GORGEOUS?

YOW!! IT'S BY BELINDA BUTWINK OF LOS ANGELES, CALIFORNIA!! SHE COVERED ME WITH MORE MAKE-UP THAN CYNDI LAUPER!

YOUR ZIPPY DOLL IS IN TH' MAIL!!

Panel 2:
BELINDA SAYS HER "GOAL IN LIFE IS TO HAVE A CAREER IN HAIR DESIGN".. A WORTHY AMBITION, I MIGHT ADD! .. SECOND THROUGH FIFTH PRIZES (ZIPPY CALENDARS) GO OUT TO:

MY GOAL IN LIFE IS TO BE NAMED BELINDA BUTWINK..

- BOBBIE VAN SLEET (BOSTON)
- J. OYARZO HICKEY (PALO ALTO)
- JEFF STEVENS (PEABODY MA.)
- SETH FEINBERG (BROOKLINE MA.)

INTERNATIONAL SOCIETY OF TASTE ARBITERS

Panel 3:
SIXTH THROUGH TENTH PRIZES (ZIPPY BOOKS) GO TO:

- RUTH WAYTZ (W. HOLLYWOOD CA.)
- JOHN ROHRER (WESTMINSTER MD.)
- JAMES MOLIS (BOSTON)
- JIM CLOW (VANCOUVER WA.)
- FRANK DAVIS (AURORA CO.)

YOU'RE ALL BEAUTIFUL DUDES & DUDESSES & I MEAN THAT FROM TH' BOTTOM OF MY BABY-BLUE BOXER SHORTS!

1-16

ZIPPY

"PERPLEXAS"

BILL GRIFFITH

Panel 1:
ZIPPY, YOU'RE IN TEXAS NOW AND YOU HAVE TO DECIDE WHICH HAT YOU'LL BE WEARING !!

HATS? ARE THEY FROM "SID'S LIDS 'N STUFF" AT TH' "GALLERIA"?

BUD

Panel 2:
AMAZING! NOTHING BUT INTER-CONNECTED MALLS FOR 85 MILES.. THIS IS AMERICA, ZIP.. TH' HEARTLAND, WHERE TH' DEER & TH' ANTELOPE SHOP !!

SO MANY "ARBEY'S" AND SO LITTLE TIME--

1-19

Panel 3:
TH' LANGUAGE IS A LOT MORE COLORFUL, TOO.. A TRUE TEXAS ACCENT IS A WONDER TO BEHOLD !!

GOL-DANG IT!! DAD-BLAST IT!! GOL-DURN IT!! DAG-NAB IT AN' HANG TEN !!

Panel 4:
I S'POSE SOONER OR LATER, TH' WHOLE COUNTRY'LL BE ONE VAST "METROPLEX"!

WILLIE NELSON ALREADY OWNS MY BUILDING !!

CONDOS TO GO

SONIC FOOD

WATER SLIDE

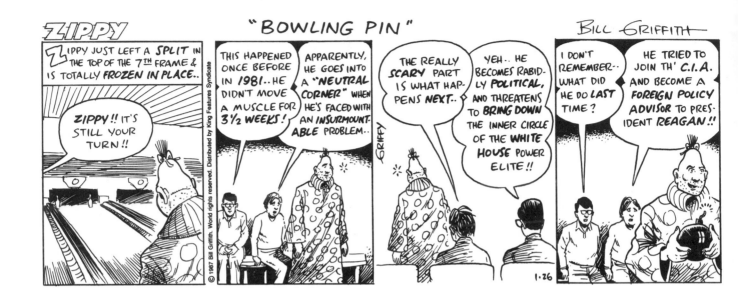

ZIPPY "WHO, WHAT, WHERE, WHEN & WHY" BILL GRIFFITH

ZIPPY SAILS THROUGH THE OZONE ON HIS **FLYING PEPPERONI PIZZA**...

YOW!! I'M HIGH ABOVE THE "**RASCAL HOUSE**" DELI IN **MIAMI, FLORIDA**!!

VERONICA, DARLING, IT'S NOT POSSIBLE THAT A **PIZZA** COULD BE **FLYING** OVER MIAMI, IS IT, DARLING??

ANYTHING IS POSSIBLE IN THIS **FERSHLUGGINER** CRAZY WORLD TODAY, MARVIN...

...I WOULD LIKE TO BE **ON** THAT PIZZA, DARLING...WITH A **FULL HEAD** OF **HAIR** AND A FRESHLY LAUNDERED **TERRY-CLOTH BATHROBE**...

PASS ME THE **SOUR TOMATOES**, MARVIN...

 ZIPPY "WARM, GENTLE, INNOCENT" BILL GRIFFITH

DID I EVER TELL YOU ABOUT MY **IMAGINARY FRIEND**??

SHE APPEARS TO ME IN MOMENTS OF **STRESS** & **SELF-DOUBT**...

HER NAME IS "**LOUISE LUDVIG**"... SAY A FEW **WORDS**, HONEY!!

HA, HA, HA... LOUISE, YOU'RE **INCORRIGIBLE**!!

2·25

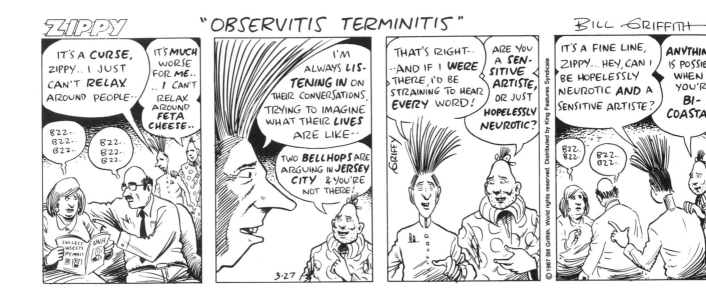

ZIPPY "EXECUTIVE MATERIAL" BILL GRIFFITH

THIS IS MY NEW FRIEND, LIONEL... HE'S A CORPORATE EXECUTIVE!!

I HAVE A LARGE DESK AND A SMALL SECRETARY!!

A CORPORATE EXEC, HUH? WHAT EXACTLY DO YOU DO, LIONEL?

4.2

TELL HIM EXACTLY WHAT YOU DO, LIONEL!!

WELL, I ORGANIZE CONSOLIDATED OPINION FOR MAXIMIZED AVAILABILITY OF COORDINATED ACCESS--

SOUNDS IMPORTANT.. ..WHAT D'YOU THINK OF THIS REVEALING PHOTO OF MORGAN BRITTANY?

WELL?

SHE'S A LOVELY LADY, ISN'T SHE, LIONEL?

CAN I GET BACK TO YOU ON THAT NEXT THURSDAY ??

ZIPPY "SHADOW BOXING" BILL GRIFFITH

I'M FEELING DRAMATICALLY LIT TODAY--

I'M INTO A KIND OF MOODY PLAY OF LIGHT & SHADOW...

WHY IS THAT, ZIP?

...MY SET'S BEING REPAIRED--

4.3

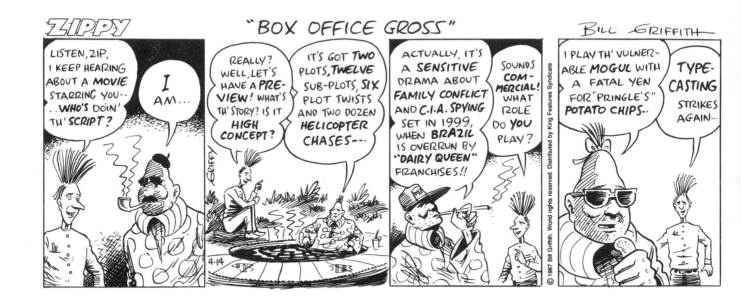

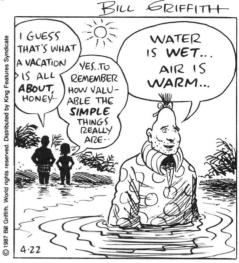

ZIPPY "CELL MEETING" BILL GRIFFITH

THIS **CELLULAR PHONE** CRAZE IS TRULY **PATHETIC!!** MUST WE BE **PLUGGED** INTO EACH OTHER AT **ALL** TIMES? WHATEVER HAPPENED TO THAT **CALM, STILL VOICE** INSIDE??

YOU'LL HAVE TO SPEAK **LOUDER,** GRIFFY...

...MY **CALM, STILL VOICE** INSIDE IS SHOUTING **PORK FUTURES** ORDERS TO TH' **CALM, STILL VOICE** OF MY INVESTMENT BANKER!!

GONNA BE LATE FOR DINNER...

GOOD..I FORGOT TO CALL IT IN...

4-28

© 1987 Bill Griffith. World rights reserved. Distributed by King Features Syndicate

---

 ZIPPY "A DOG'S LIFE" BILL GRIFFITH

STARHOUND! WHAT'S TH' **MATTER?** YOU HAVEN'T **SNIFFED** A **CELEBRITY** SINCE **CHARO'S** BIRTHDAY!!

I'M EXAMINING MY **MOTIVES,** ZIPPY..I'M NOT SURE I WANT TO SPEND MY LIFE **NOSE-DEEP** IN **MORGAN BRIT- TANY'S** BATH TOWELS!!

4-29

BUT, **STAR- HOUND,** YOUR **NOSTRILS** ARE TH' **PLAYTHINGS** OF TH' **RICH & FAMOUS!!**

I THINK I'M SUFFERING FROM WHAT **FREUD** CALLS A "DISPLACE- MENT **NEUROSIS,"** ZIP.. I SHIFT MY **OWN** PROBLEMS ONTO **BURT REYNOLDS'** PERSONA...

...THEN I MAKE **FUN** OF POOR **BURT** AS A WAY OF DENYING THOSE SAME TRAITS IN **MYSELF!!** DON'T YOU SEE? I CAN'T STAND MY OWN **STINK!**

ISN'T THAT TH' LOVELY HOTEL QUEEN, **LEONA HELMSLEY,** SIPPING A DAIQUIRI AT TH' NEXT TABLE?

IT'S NO USE, ZIPPY-- MY **NOSE** IS IN **NEUTRAL**..IT WILL NO LONGER SERVE TH' **TWISTED NEEDS** OF AN IMMATURE PSYCHE--

LEONA! **SMIRK** AT ME !! PLEASE!!

© 1987 Bill Griffith. World rights reserved. Distributed by King Features Syndicate

ZIPPY

"WATERY DISSOLVE"

BILL GRIFFITH

WE NEED A **DIRECTOR** FOR YOUR **MOVIE**, ZIPPY.. ...FELLINI'S BUSY, SCORCESE'S GOT TH' FLU...I'M IN A **QUANDARY**..

IF IT'S A **CHINESE** QUANDARY, I'D LIKE MY SHORTS STEAMED AND PRESSED!!

5·6

FILM IS A LOT LIKE **COMICS**, ZIP... THEY'VE BOTH GOT **ONE** FOOT IN TH' WORLD OF **COMMERCE** & **ONE** FOOT IN TH' WORLD OF **ART**!!

DON'T FORGET TH' ONE IN THEIR **MOUTH**!

WHY DON'T YOU DIRECT IT **YOURSELF**? AFTER ALL, YOU USED TO SELL **VINYL SEAT COVERS**!!

YOU THINK I COULD? IT'S A THOUGHT. ..I'D NEED A PAIR OF **SUN-GLASSES**, A **BULL-HORN**, A **CLIP-BOARD**...

CAN I HAVE MY **OSCAR** WITH EXTRA **MUSTARD**, HOLD TH' **MAYO**??

LIGHTS!! CAMERA!! **NON-LINEAR ACTION!!**

CITIZEN ZIPPY

ZIPPY

"THAT'S ENTERTAINMENT"

BILL GRIFFITH

THE RAIN WHIPPED THROUGH THE CITY STREETS LIKE A MOODY, TECHNICALLY EFFECTIVE METAPHOR, SUGGESTING "A **MAN** ON A **MISSION**"--

CAMERA ANGLES WERE EMPLOYED TO FURTHER ENHANCE INSTANT VIEWER **INVOLVEMENT** IN THE SCENE..

SILHOUETTES CONVEYED A DRAMATIC, **MYSTERIOUS** QUALITY TO THE ENIGMATIC FIGURE---

IN THE LAST SHOT, A **SPOT-LIGHT** WAS USED TO EMPHASIZE THE FACT THAT THERE WAS NO **CONTENT** TO THE SEQUENCE & THAT IT WAS SIMPLY A SERIES OF SLICK, "HIGH-CONCEPT" **VISUAL EFFECTS**..

HI.. MY NAME IS JOE ISUZU..

5·7

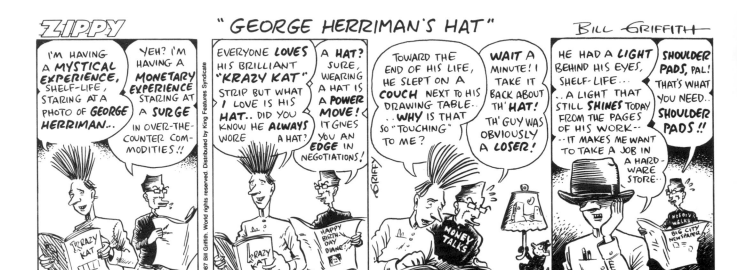

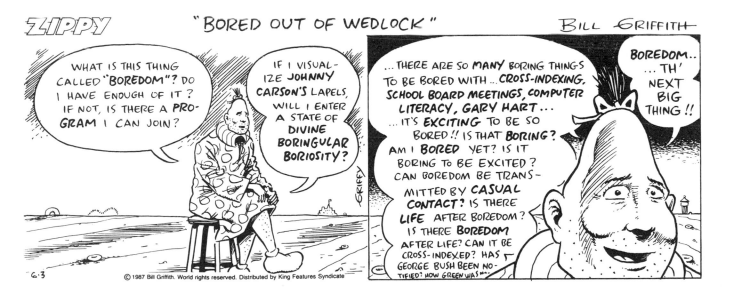

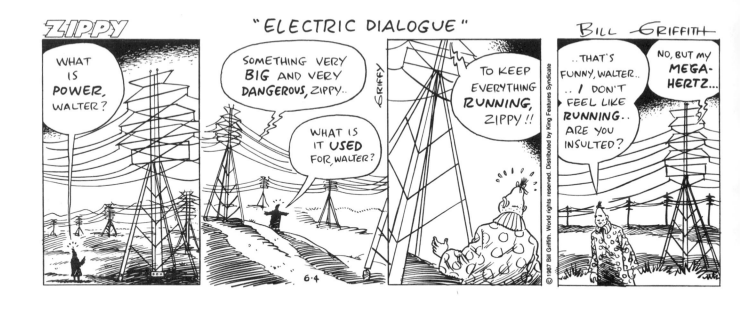

ZIPPY "PEDESTRIAN EXPERIENCE" BILL GRIFFITH

© 1987 Bill Griffith. World rights reserved. Distributed by King Features Syndicate

6·16

UH-OH... I'VE COME TO A MAJOR **CROSSWALK** IN LIFE -- DO I **YIELD**... OR PREPARE TO **MERGE**??

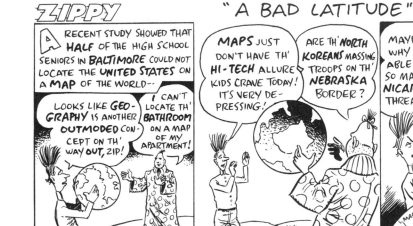

ZIPPY "A BAD LATITUDE" BILL GRIFFITH

A RECENT STUDY SHOWED THAT **HALF** OF THE HIGH SCHOOL SENIORS IN **BALTIMORE** COULD NOT LOCATE THE **UNITED STATES** ON A MAP OF THE WORLD--

LOOKS LIKE **GEOGRAPHY** IS ANOTHER **OUTMODED** CONCEPT ON TH' WAY OUT, ZIP!

I CAN'T LOCATE TH' **BATHROOM** ON A MAP OF MY APARTMENT!

MAPS JUST DON'T HAVE TH' **HI-TECH** ALLURE KIDS CRAVE TODAY! IT'S VERY DEPRESSING!

ARE TH' **NORTH KOREANS** MASSING TROOPS ON TH' **NEBRASKA** BORDER?

6·17

MAYBE THAT'S WHY **REAGAN'S** ABLE TO CONVINCE SO MANY PEOPLE **NICARAGUA** IS A THREAT TO TH' U.S.!

ISN'T **NICARAGUA** SOMEWHERE BETWEEN **IDAHO** & **RAPID CITY**?

SOMETIMES I THINK **AMERICA** IS LIKE A **NARCISSISTIC**, SELF-ABSORBED **TEENAGER**, ZIPPY! DOES IT WORRY YOU, TOO??

I'M WORRIED ABOUT TH' **SERBO-CROATIAN** TANKS HEADING FOR DOWNTOWN **BALTIMORE**!

© 1987 Bill Griffith. World rights reserved. Distributed by King Features Syndicate

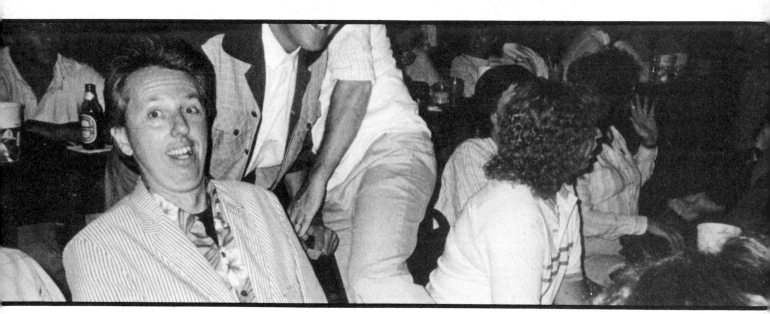

Andrew Lucas/Rocky Mountain News